Noddy and
the Driving Lesson

Collins

An Imprint of HarperCollinsPublishers

NODDY

CLOCKWORK MOUSE

BIG-EARS

MARTHA

TESSIE BEAR

GOBBO

MR PLOD

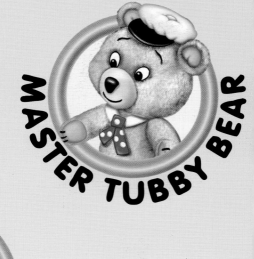

MASTER TUBBY BEAR

ONKEY

SLY

MR WOBBLY MAN

BUMPY DOG

It was a pleasant evening in Toyland . . .

Noddy was having a nice time out at the café, with Tessie Bear and Dinah Doll.

"What delicious apple pie!" Noddy said, licking his lips.

"I wish I had my own apple tree," Noddy remarked, "I'd pick apples and make pies every single day!"

They knew that Mr Straw sold apple trees but they also knew that the trees cost quite a bit of money. So they all had a think about what Noddy could do to earn a bit extra.

"I know!" Tessie exclaimed suddenly. "A lot of toys want to drive a car like you do, Noddy. Why don't you offer driving lessons to those toys? You would soon make plenty of money!"

But the next day, the first toy to whom Noddy offered
driving lessons seemed quite frightened by the idea. It
was Mr Tubby Bear, and he made all sorts of excuses!

"Oh... er... I much prefer walking," he told Noddy
quickly. "Yes... er... walking is a favourite hobby of
mine!"

Clockwork Mouse was far more keen on having driving lessons! But Noddy was not sure if letting Clockwork Mouse drive his car was such a good idea.

"I hear you're offering driving lessons, Noddy?" Clockwork Mouse asked excitedly.

"Er... yes, I suppose so," Noddy replied hesitantly.

"Now you will be careful with my little car, won't you?" Noddy implored as Clockwork Mouse jumped into the driving seat.

Noddy explained to Clockwork Mouse how to start and stop the car, and how to make it go forwards and backwards.

"You do understand everything don't you, Clockwork Mouse?" Noddy asked nervously as he showed him the gear stick.

"Oh yes! Nothing to it!" Clockwork Mouse replied.

Clockwork Mouse put his foot down on the car's pedal so that it would go forwards.

But he had not been listening properly to Noddy and instead of going forwards, the car jumped backwards!

Clockwork Mouse at last managed to make the car go forwards. But he drove it too fast, swerving all over the place!

"Look out!" Noddy cried, grabbing the steering wheel, as they nearly crashed into a wall.

Soon they approached Stony Bridge, Noddy still ordering Clockwork Mouse to slow down.

"Whee-ee!" Clockwork Mouse cried with delight as the car leapt off the bridge into the air. "Aren't I brilliant? I can fly as well as drive!"

At last the driving lesson was over and Noddy staggered out of his car, shaking like a leaf.

"Well, that was your first lesson!" he panted, wiping his brow.

"Thank you," said Clockwork Mouse, "I'm a brilliant driver now, so I shan't need any more lessons!"

Noddy was quite delighted that Clockwork Mouse did not want any more driving lessons. Indeed, he really wished that he did not have to give lessons to any of the toys. It made him far too nervous!

But Noddy still desperately wanted to buy an apple tree. "Would you like to learn to drive?" he asked Jumbo.

But Jumbo said he was far too big to squeeze into the little car, so Noddy offered his services to Sammy Sailor.

"Would you like a driving lesson, Sammy?" he asked.

"Oh no, young Noddy!" Sammy replied. "Car driving is not for the likes of us sea-faring folk!"

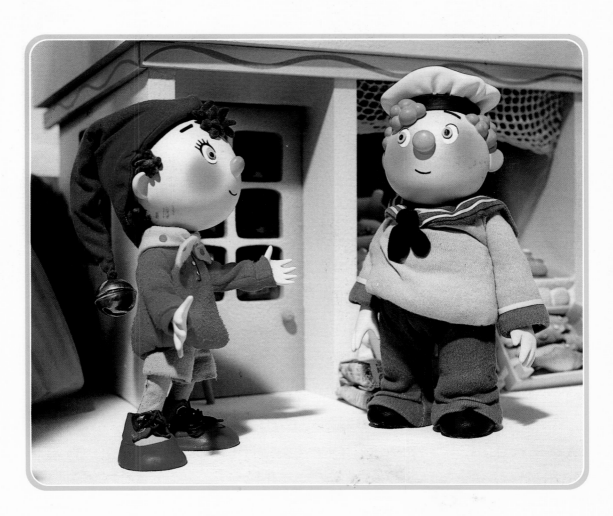

Next, Noddy tried to persuade Big-Ears to have driving lessons.

"Oh, no thank you, Noddy," Big-Ears replied. "Riding a bicycle is quite enough for me!"

Noddy was so sad. "Whatever am I going to do?" he sighed. "Oh, I'll never make enough sixpences to buy an apple tree!"

While Noddy was away from his car, Clockwork Mouse looked at it very enviously.

"I wish I dared borrow Noddy's car," he said to himself out loud.

"You can't drive!" said a snivelling voice behind him. It was Sly, the naughty goblin!

"Yes I can drive!" Clockwork Mouse told Sly and Gobbo proudly. "I'm a brilliant driver. Noddy taught me. He wants to buy an apple tree from Mr Straw's farm so he's giving driving lessons to earn lots of money!"

All this made Gobbo think up a wicked plan. He decided to pinch some of Mr Straw's apple trees and sell them to the toys himself. All he needed to do was to trick Clockwork Mouse into collecting the trees for him!

"We've got some collecting to do, Sly," Gobbo said, turning to him craftily. "I wish we knew a brilliant driver..."

"I'll be your brilliant driver!" Clockwork Mouse offered at once.

"But you don't have a car," said Gobbo, winking at Sly.

"We could borrow Noddy's car!" Clockwork Mouse exclaimed.

Poor Noddy! He was so upset when he came back to his car and found that it was gone.

"My lovely car!" he wailed to Mr Plod. "Someone's stolen it!"

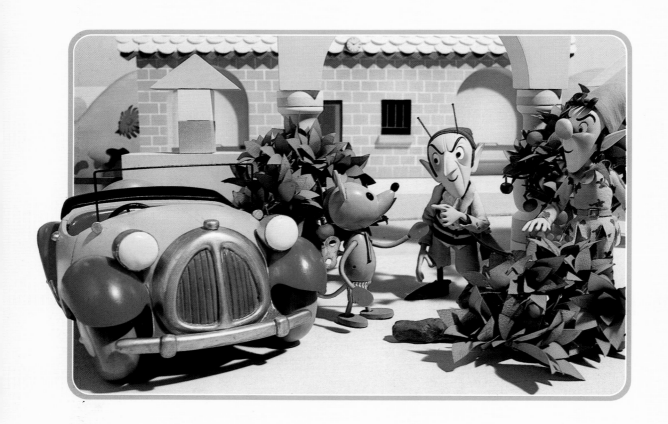

Clockwork Mouse drove the goblins to Mr Straw's farm, where they secretly dug up some of his apple trees. Then he took them to the station so they could sell the trees to passers-by.

By now, though, Clockwork Mouse was starting to become a bit suspicious.

"Are you sure Mr Straw gave you his permission to sell his apple trees?" he asked.

"Yes of course he did!" Gobbo snapped. "Now get off with you. We don't need you any more!"

Noddy's car was quite a clever little car and it knew Sly and Gobbo were up to no good. So while the goblins were selling one of the apple trees to Mr Sparks, the car made its escape!

Meanwhile, Clockwork Mouse was feeling so bad about helping the goblins that he went and told everything to Noddy and Mr Plod.

But before Mr Plod could begin looking for clues, Big-Ears arrived with some good news for them all. He had found Noddy's car and it was perfectly safe!

Just at that moment, Mr Sparks arrived carrying the apple tree the goblins had sold to him.

"I'll take charge of that!" Mr Plod barked just as Mr Sparks was about to give the tree to Miss Pink Cat as a gift.

"Did you purchase this apple tree from Gobbo and Sly?"
Mr Plod asked sternly.

"Well... yes..." Mr Sparks replied nervously.

"Well, I'm afraid that tree is a stolen tree!" Mr Plod announced, looking more fearsome than ever. "I shall go straightaway and arrest those goblins. Firstly, for stealing Mr Straw's trees and secondly, for stealing Noddy's car!"

"Remember telling me how much you wanted your very own apple tree?" Big-Ears asked when they were back at Noddy's house. "Well, if you plant this magic apple that's exactly what you will have!"

"Why is it magic?" Noddy asked curiously.

"Just wait until tomorrow and see!" was all that Big-Ears would say.

Noddy could hardly sleep that night. He kept wondering what was so magical about the apple.

As soon as morning dawned, he jumped out of bed and dashed to the window.

Noddy could not believe his eyes...

The magic apple had grown into a tree overnight!

"I can make as many apple pies as I want now!" he laughed happily.

This edition first published in Great Britain by HarperCollins Publishers Ltd in 2000

1 3 5 7 9 10 8 6 4 2

Copyright © 1999 Enid Blyton Ltd. Enid Blyton's signature mark and the words
"NODDY" and "TOYLAND" are Registered Trade Marks of Enid Blyton Ltd.
For further information on Enid Blyton please contact www.blyton.com

ISBN: 0 00 136185 6

Reproduction by Graphic Studio S.r.l. Verona
Printed in Italy by Garzanti Verga S.r.l.

MORE NODDY BOOKS FOR YOU TO ENJOY

Noddy and the Artists

Noddy and the Bouncing Ball

Noddy is Caught in a Storm

Noddy is Far Too Busy

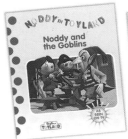

Noddy and the Goblins

Noddy and the Magic Watch

Noddy and the Noisy Drum

Noddy the Nurse

Noddy and the Singing Bush

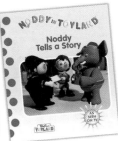

Noddy Tells a Story

Noddy Tidies Toyland

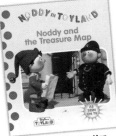

Noddy and the Treasure Map